THE OTHER:
Volume 3 of Penny

Kate Thomas Wood / Editor, Art Director
Katia Diamond-Sagias / Assistant Editor
Plum / Guest Art Director
Mitucami Mituca / Guest Editor
Richard Fraser / Guest Editor
Aparna Datey / Staff Reader
Jack Feerick / Staff Reader
Yadira Lopez / Staff Reader
Maeve MacLysaght / Staff Reader
Marissa Sammy / Staff Reader
You / Reader, Commenter
Cover illustration by DefinitelyJenny

PENNY, EXPERIMENTS IN ILLUSTRATED PROSE, IS PUBLISHED BY SIXPENNY & CO. PUBLISHING, LLC, SARASOTA, FL, 34231. NO PART OF THIS PUBLICATION MAY BE REPRODUCED, STORED IN A RETRIEVAL SYSTEM, OR TRANSMITTED IN ANY FORM OR BY ANY MEANS, ELECTRONIC, MECHANICAL, PHOTOCOPYING, RECORDING, OR OTHERWISE, WITHOUT THE PRIOR WRITTEN PERMISSION OF SIXPENNY & CO. PUBLISHING, LLC. VISIT OUR WEBSITE AT WWW.PENNYZINE.CO. IF YOU ARE A RETAILER AND WOULD LIKE TO ORDER PENNY, PLEASE EMAIL KATE@SIXPENNY.ORG. THIS IS IN ALL CAPS BECAUSE THAT'S WHAT EVERYONE ELSE DOES.

ISBN 9780997537222

NO. 003, PRINTED FEBRUARY 2018

💻 www.pennyzine.co | 🅕 sixpennyco
🅞 @penny_zine | 🅘 @youfoundpenny

EDITORS' NOTE

Welcome to the third volume (and first bookazine) of our ongoing experiment with illustrated prose at *Penny*. One year ago, we chose 'The Other' as the theme for this collection. Trump had won the election and we grappled with an urgent question: How could we support marginalized communities with our limited personal resources?

Thinking that a greater understanding of 'otherness' would foster empathy across borders small and large, we began by calling for submissions that considered the feeling of otherness within, as well as explorations of what it means to be pushed to the margins by a dominant culture.

However, we faced a limitation of perspective—as a self-selected group of friends we have much in common. So we put out a call for staff readers, and asked that anyone interested apply by telling us their best idea for a submission prompt on the theme of 'The Other.' The authors of the most insightful prompts joined us in shaping this volume and became our readers. They come from all over the world and range from journalist to teacher of architectural design, from comics artist to secretary at a mental health clinic. They are awesome, busy people, who spent several hours each week for months reading blind submissions.

We also asked Plum, an illustration collective in Brooklyn, to art direct and illustrate four of the stories. They decided to do their own experiment and collectively illustrated those stories. Amazing, unknowable things occurred.

This volume is the product of over 30 voices coming together to notice, to reveal, and to raise up some of what has been hidden. The stories within these pages explore the anger, celebration, wariness, curiosity, repulsion and attraction humans can have for otherness—a surprisingly large scope.

In the back of this volume, you will find a list of QR codes and shortened URLs. This is not because the robots have taken over. Not yet. If you choose one of these methods of input for your internet-enabled device, you will be taken to the online home of each of these stories, where we invite you to add your comments and ideas. We look forward to hearing from you.

CONTENTS

CAFÉ

Fiction

Illustrated by Mitucami Mituca
Written by David Mohan

We walk in out of the cold, Donata and I.

It is November, but Carlo's always has a hint of August. We queue up behind two fur-hatted ladies, pointing out pastries. We don't speak. We're sleepy. We have come from a late night showing of *Double Indemnity*, and are too dazzled by noir to speak.

'Just a drink,' Donata has suggested, 'and something sweet, and I shall be ready for bed.'

The cappuccino machine whirrs, clicks and sings. It sends out a deep hiss, a musky sound, as resonant as something from the throat of a big cat. The air is sugar-scented, the trays are loaded with bite-size confections, aspic red jellies on circlets of biscotti, dabs of meringue, blobs and swirls of chocolate.

The coffee machine spits out a frothy cough and we turn our heads to the zinc counter.

When it is our turn, Donata orders an espresso and two miniature meringues. I

Coffee
detox

order a cappuccino and a lemon slice. We need sugar—it's winter after all, and we've just seen the world revealed to us in black and white, a bitter place governed by money and lust.

We sit on two high stools at a small, circular table beside the window. Outside is blurred by snow flurries. It looks distant and romantic.

We don't speak. Our eyes meet and we are of the same mind. We are still in the world of our film. This happens sometimes—there needs to be a place like this, a café or restaurant, a street corner or metro train. You need to find somewhere to decompress, let reality flood back, piece by piece.

Donata sits erect, a femme fatale, holds her cup to her lips, sips. A film can give you that level of poise. I sit back, attempting to look disenchanted. It can be hard out in the cold working without a script. I tear the corner of my paper napkin.

It seems the whole world waits for my next gesture.

 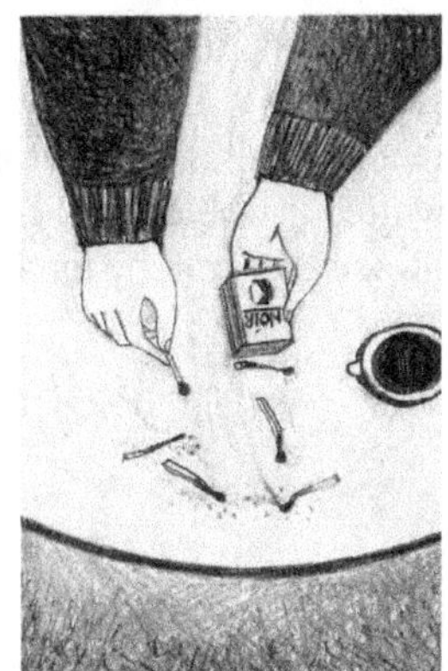

We are on the cusp of boredom, but even boredom in the long light cast by our film has possibilities. Donata dabs her mouth daintily and then with a grave expression re-applies her lipstick. Then she pouts at the keyhole of her reflection in her compact. I play my fingers across the table-top, itching for cigarettes.

Outside is Milan, the future, non-fiction, waiting for us.

Soon, we will be finished, the taste of coffee
and sugar will dissolve in our mouths, and
we will walk across town to our train, the
whiteout of the snow like a screen run out
to its last, scratchy loop.

DEAR NNAMDI

Fiction

Illustrated by Plum
Written by Tyrese L. Coleman

Sent: Sat 8/15/2015 6:03 AM

I shouldn't show up today, but I'm coming to your wedding. The *American* wedding. I will stand when the minister asks if anyone objects because I do, and I've always wanted to attend a wedding where that happens. I'm a law student, I know how to object. I've got evidence to sustain. Your poems. Dick-pics. Clothes in my dresser. Toothbrush in my bathroom. Morning calls. Morning wood. You. Here. Sleeping. Now.

Maybe I am a whore like your mother thinks.

But my bed is warm, body still slick and tender.

Maybe we made a baby.

Sent: Sat 8/15/2015 11:28 AM

Just so you know, I don't care about *Miss Nigeria.* The opposite of me with her bright cocoa skin, flawless weave, make-up expertly applied. Yes, I know what she looks like—saved your picture from the Metro Section. *Two doctors, first generation, prominent families, two weddings—here and in Nigeria—homes in D.C., London, Lagos.* Tell your Igbo-bougie mother you taught me how to make fufu. My southern accent doesn't mean I'm stupid, just as much as her being asked to repeat herself because her words start with O's wide like butts in Kente cloth doesn't mean shit either.

1. I will be an attorney. A judge! 2. You were my first, my only. 3. My father is a professor, my mother a chef, my sister a nurse. 4. I am a good woman.

But—Miss Nigeria is Igbo.

Congratulations. You found a suitable wife.

Your precious mother hates the sight of me. I'm impure, I know, I know. My best friend says light-skin women have nothing to complain about. She pulls my hair like I'm a doll, tells me I need a tan: my legs are Perdue chicken thighs. That shit ain't funny. My yellow-brown thighs signal wantonness, physical proof of brown legs split for a white dick—you know—we talked about that. Late night, ganja filled our chests, and

we pontificated: Ann Petry's *The Street,* the sex-crazed mulatta tragedy of Sara Jane in *Imitation of Life.* Literature doesn't provide happy endings for women who look like me. Real life doesn't either. That night you told me about her. Said she didn't matter. Appease your mother, you said. Does Miss Nigeria know your poetry? The idleness of writing doesn't seem to fit your mother's ideal of a good Igbo boy. She hates the influence of my pale otherness on you, yet I know nothing but black.

Black not African.

"Never African. Never Nigerian. Never Igbo. Never for you." Your mother chastened when we met as if you were a child bringing home a stray dog.

But on some western shore, my ancestor was sister to her ancestor, and they stole mine. I'm no longer littered with sand, not enough grit to grip when the boat leaves, and we are tied feet to wrist. This will get me in trouble, but I speak what's in my bones. It's our bones from another lifetime, Nnamdi, lying at the sea bottom. If you marry her, they will never make it home.

This is not an apology.

I handled myself well. Had your mother not put her finger in my face—her sculpted head wrap quivering with each chicken-like neck jerk—if she had just sat down like the lady she claims, if she had not called me *aka-ta* with her nose wrinkled like she smelled shit, or like I was shit, and what was I doing there, and who the hell did I think I was, then I may not have had to raise my voice and tell the church where you were at 6:03 AM. I know you said that word doesn't mean *nigger,* but that's how she said it. I know! If anyone out of us is a nigger, it's me.

I am not begging you to take me back.

But, when she slapped me, was there any part of you that wanted to act? My face cracked, red, glowed with tears and blood vessels. You watched while every woman there spat in my face, your male cousins laughing, high-fiving behind your back. Did your heart stir? Eight years, and you can't protect me?

Friends warned me about Nigerian men. We've all dated at least one, a black woman's rite of passage. It's ignorant to generalize. Not *all* Nigerian men are like you. But, you don't make it easy. Or is it just men? That's what Amy Winehouse is singing to me. We staring down this dark liquid tunnel numbing my face, my body, what's left of my mind. What is it about men? *What iis it abboouut men?* Amy and I, we commiserating.

I saw the real you at the altar. Beautiful—no doubt, that's why I love you. The ceremony in a golden dusky light, you were an eclipse. In you seeing her, I didn't perceive romantic love. Nah. Greater. Greater than what I thought we had. I see it now. Saw it when you cried at the sight of her—pride instead of love. Your heart sang some language I don't understand. Pride greater than any love you could ever have for me. I have no culture. I come from plain old slavery and miscegenation. She's your lifelong dream. Of dances and song and food and family and hope and everything else. She's your mother, and her mother, and her mother. She's the reason why you're here. The reason I fell for you. And for you...I could never be for you.

I'll take a wash for the past eight years

and just say I'll see you next lifetime. Maybe then we will both make it through the middle passage. Or not. I've got work tomorrow. Come get your shit.

End.

THE FREE CLINIC

Creative Nonfiction

Illustrated by Chrissy Curtin
Written by Katy Shay

When I was sixteen, she asked me to go
with her, to the free clinic in the county
building, to sit on a hard plastic chair with
her and wait and wait. Her chair would be
orange and mine would be green, and we
would wait for as long as it took. The sun
was setting on the latter half of the nineties.
It was starting to get late.

When we were six we had sleepovers,
camped out in bags on her living room
floor. Her mom had two angels crafted out
of plastic beads and wire. There was a blue
angel and a red angel. I liked the red angel;
the beads hard crystals that refracted light.
I wanted to crush them between my
teeth but could not.
When it was time to go to sleep I put
the red angel by my side. Then I tossed and
turned on top of the angel crushing it with
the tiny cavity of my six-year-old chest. The
angel popped and beads scattered.
I picked one up and stuck it in my
mouth.
The next day her mom hollered at the
both of us. Me for breaking it, her for letting
me do it.

In the lobby of the free clinic in the county building on the absolute edge of our midwestern town, we sat in those two hard chairs. Somehow she was old enough to drive, somehow she had a car, somehow she'd lost her virginity before me and neither of us knew what to do so we just sat there, waiting for her to be seen.

I think she was happy about it, if not freaked out in the way that you might be when you engage in consensual vaginal penetration for the first and you look at your partner and think, "You've been inside of me."

There are so many other ways that this can go down.

It was the nineties and her favorite band was The Smashing Pumpkins and mine was Nirvana. She loved Nirvana, too, but I never wanted to hear her say it because I was so weird and possessive.

We weren't as close as we had been as kids. We didn't lie to strangers any more and say we are sisters and refer to each other as "Sis" or "Sissy." We didn't talk in our made up language. We didn't stay up until three am together anymore laughing hysterically over the word piss. We no longer planned to marry twins and live in mansions right next door to one another.

She was quiet sitting on that hard chair in the clinic in the county building on the edge of the town, the hard edge of the millennium. They finally gave her some forms to fill out. Family history, sexual history, emotional history, a questionnaire of what she'd experienced thus far?

Had she been hit/yelled at/told where and when to go/ told that he'll kill himself if you leave, he'll really fucking do it? Has he ever: grabbed your tit in the harsh light of the halls of your suburban high school/ vaginally penetrated you when you said no, no, no/ locked you in the laundry room with him and made you watch while he jerked himself off?

How could I sit there with her and not know the answer to those questions?

She had no idea what to do with her hair back then.

It was getting dark. The millennium was about to turn over and under the shadow of the second Bush administration the clinic would be shut down. We sat, waited for her name to be called, for her to be taken into the back to sit on that crinkly paper, scratching at her thighs.

I hope our hands dangled, like when we were little girls. While she checked off boxes, I hope my hand found hers. I hope I laced my fingers in and held on.

BETWEEN THE WISH AND THE THING

Creative Nonfiction

Illustrated by Franz Lang
Written by Jess E. Jelsma
and Matt Jones

When you have an affair, you learn to speak in a coded language only the two of you can understand.

Out in public, you tell your colleagues that the two of you have become "close friends." That you are strictly platonic confidantes. That your connection is akin to a brother/sister bond. That your conversations are equal parts vapid college anecdotes, light-hearted work gossip, and generic commiseration. That even if there was more there, you don't even find each other attractive.

At home, you tell your husband that you need someone to talk to about your flailing marriage. That the other man is too pretty and effeminate to be a real threat. That, after months of getting to know one another, you think of him as stupid and arrogant. That the other man is little more than a nice-looking sounding board to bounce ideas off. That even if there was something there, a man like him would never be attracted to someone as emotionally beat down and self-conscious as you.

Even around one another, the topic is one you never directly address. You speak to each other in vague hypotheticals and swap stories that always seem to center the narrative around other relationships. You talk about awkward first kisses, blind dates gone horribly wrong, and the odd sexual proclivities of former partners. When you do discuss your desires and attractions, the gaze is always directed at someone else. Aidan Turner. Ciara. Taylor Lautner. A mutual colleague.

You leave these conversations feeling frustrated, hot-faced, and angry.

In public and private, however, your body language tells a different story. At the bar, you stand so close to one another that, to others, your bodies appear fused from the shoulders to the hips. You share bottles of Bud Light and swap bites of cheap, overcooked game day hot dogs. You find whatever ways you can to swap spit. Shared bananas. Passed slices of greasy pizza. Alternating pulls off a water bottle filled with vanilla vodka.

So when the question finally does comes up—yet another childish, truth-or-dare hypothetical—the words should feel inevitable.

You lay your forearms on the other man's pock-mocked kitchen table and ask, "What would you do if I tried to kiss you?"

Because you've learned that, in the coded language of affairs, the only way he can answer is with a physical response.

. . .

When you have an affair, you begin to hear stories that you did not tell. Sometimes just about her, and sometimes about the two of you, and other times about all three of you together.

Someone says that you are all swingers. That you get off on watching each other.

Another person says that you and her are exhibitionists. If you aren't fucking inside of the windmill that marks hole 12 at the local putt-putt golf course on Route 69, then you're fucking in the library. In the bathrooms of the empty football stadium. On the quad in front of the birds and the group tours the university gives to potential students.

Everyone always assumes that you're fucking. People think you are slowly winding your way through the canon of iconic Hollywood adultery: Julia Roberts and Jude Law in *Closer*, Kate Winslet and Patrick Wilson in *Little Children*, Diane Lane and Olivier Martinez in *Unfaithful*. When you have an affair, you think of the casual way with which Richard Gere's character in *Unfaithful* picked up a snow globe and bashed in the head of the other man who had been sleeping with his wife. When you tell your mom about the affair, not in those words—instead you confess that you are simply in love with a married woman—she asks if her husband owns a gun. If he is an angry person. If he might cause you any harm.

You assure her that this man owns no guns. His body is narrow and soft. You have envisioned—sometimes fantasized—on too many occasions what it would be like to confront him—to have it out with him—whatever that means. When you have an affair, you are sometimes consumed by desires of different sorts.

You never refute the stories that you hear about the two of you. Not because they are true, but because you are tired. So is she. After all, who has time for rebuttal, or refutation, or explanation, or apology? Who has time for confession or justification? Not you two, of course. After all, you're so caught up in each other, what with all the exhibitionism and the sneaking around and the fucking like banshees across the Bible Belt. Or so you hear. So you have been told.

. . .

When you have an affair, you are driven by bodily needs and a set of latent, previously undetected instincts.

Not by the desire to stray or fuck or be wanted by some new man fresh out of his cardboard, shrink-wrapped packaging. Not by jealously, or insecurity, or any of those other motives that so many movies and TV shows have led you to believe. But by the need to breathe. To break the surface after four years of being forcefully held beneath the waves. Of existing in a state of suspended animation, your heart rate slowed and the blood vessels in your limbs constricted to direct all flow of oxygen to your brain. Of being drowned—for all intents and purposes—but not yet dead.

Your body steps in to take the lead on every movement and decision. Your hand gracefully lifting your low-ball glass to your lips when the three of you sit down together at a bar. Your face stoic and unblinking when your husband shakes an all-too-familiar t-shirt in your direction and starts shouting questions. Your hands steady on the steering wheel as you drive back home from the other man's house in the rundown part of town. Your voice calm and de-escalating as your husband shoves his hand down your underwear and says, "Remember. This is mine. Not yours."

At your in-laws house for Thanksgiving, you sleep for eighteen hours straight. You hibernate right through breakfast and early-morning football and the first matinee showings of *Skyfall* and *Lincoln*. During dinner, you are straight-faced and demure as your husband weaves elaborate lies about your life together. How well you are both adjusting to your nascent marriage. How there may be a dog or a home purchase in the near future. How many good friends you have both made at your new program.

You stare straight ahead without

STILL AT
WORK...
WILL BE
HOME
SOON

thought or comment. You bring your glass of wine to you mouth. Let the expensive Pinot Grigio sit on your palette. Carefully swallow the liquid down.

Later, when your husband tries to push apart your legs while you are sleeping, you wake up just in time to elbow him in the stomach.

At every turn and juncture, you always seem to know what you are doing. Gone is the part of your brain that is meant to second-guess your actions, your frontal lobe stored elsewhere for safekeeping. You are all cerebellum and brainstem. Pons. Medulla. Midbrain. An unconscious series of reactions. Asleep vs. awake. Inhale and exhale. Pain sensitivity. Heart rate.

With the other man, you are aggressive, cocksure, and brazen because this, your body tells you, is what the situation necessitates.

With your husband, you are cruel, dishonest, and unapologetic because this, your gut keeps reminding you, is the dog-eat-dog arena of heartbreak. Causalities are expected when one is determined to claw their way back up to the surface.

When you have an affair, you occasionally spend time with her and her husband.

You're friends—kind of—you and her husband. In a parallel universe, you might even be good friends. Groomsmen at each other's weddings. But parallel universes don't exist—at least not as far as you know—and yet, somehow, here you both are, married to the same woman at the exact same time even if only one of you knows it.

It's a fucking paradox, really. Mary Shelley says, "The silence of midnight, to speak truly, though apparently a paradox, rung in my ears." Mary knew something about paradoxes, and about monsters, too. Some people thought that Percy Shelley actually wrote *Frankenstein,* but he was just a minor collaborator. When you have an affair, you are sometimes Percy and sometimes the monster itself, which is all to say that sometimes you feel like a minor collaborator while other times you feel cobbled together by electricity and raw materials, alive in a way that is both thrilling and lonely.

An affair can feel a little like a horror

story. Not the blood and guts kind, but the mundane kind where the things that terrify you are the things that are normal. How when you all spend time together—you, her, and her husband—you go home at the end of each night while they climb into the same bed. That scares you, how routine it can all begin to feel, how this secret that you have begins to seem like just another organ in your body. Even Prometheus got used to the eagle that ate his liver every day while he was chained to a rock. That's actually the subtitle of Mary Shelley's *Frankenstein: A Modern Prometheus,* and when you have an affair, that's kind of what you feel like.

Every day that the routine goes on—that the three of you get together for lunch or drinks or football or whatever—you feel this secret ache and swell up in your body. It reminds you of your inflamed appendix when you were twelve.

But some nights, the husband goes to bed early, and when he does, you kiss her in the kitchen or on the couch and she carves that secret right out of you. It's both monstrous and beautiful. Strangely alive. Before you drive home, she reaches right into you

and puts it back inside your chest because
it's not quite ready to survive out in the
world just yet.

THE KING OF THE JUNGLE

Fiction

Illustrated by DefinitelyJenny
Written by Alistair Mackay

Nombulelo watches the darkness. Hours pass before insipid winter sunlight sneaks in between the sheet-metal walls of her shack. Ma'Khumalo said old people don't need much sleep but if that were the case, why is Nombulelo always so tired? Ma'Khumalo says a lot of stupid things like that. When the two of them went to church together every Sunday Ma'Khumalo buzzed with energy from the moment they met until they parted after dark. The singing didn't wear her down. The township gossip at tea afterwards didn't make her ache. It's her unwavering faith that gives her energy like that. She isn't old in the same way.

Nombulelo heaves the blankets off her chest and sits up. Cold air stings her skin and loosens her phlegm. She coughs. Her ribs hurt. She hears girls laughing outside on their way to school. Footsteps crunch along the gravel. The general hum grows louder and more indistinct, a peaceful cacophony of the living.

She strikes a match and dirty orange light flickers up from the lamp, turning the darkness into solid, ordinary things: a white mini fridge with a portable electric hot plate on top; an old desk with peeling wood-effect linoleum. At the end of her bed is a lumpy olive- green couch and beside it, on the floor, a plastic washbasin and Thembi's crate filled with dolls, crayons and the grubby stuffed tiger she loved so much.

There's maize-meal in the pot which Nombulelo heats, along with a cup of sweet, milky tea to help with the headache. The radio is playing one of her favorite hymns. A month ago the words would have made her angry but now she's too tired to feel anything. She ignores the words, hums only the melody. It still soars, still has a little magic left in it, almost lets her believe we're part of something greater.

"Morning Mama," comes her neighbor's voice outside the door. "Is there anything I can get for you in town?"

Nombulelo clicks in irritation. She needs kerosene and a tin of apricot jam, but there's nothing in her wallet but a crumpled photo of Thembi. "I'm fine," she shouts back. "Go. You'll miss your train."

She sits back down on the couch and begins massaging her swollen ankles. Her hand bumps against a bottle of brandy that's sitting on the floor and it teeters back and forth, announcing triumphantly how shameful she is. Pathetic and weak. She grabs hold of the neck. Did Eunice hear it? She'll tell Ma'Khumalo. Nombulelo wraps the bottle in a plastic bag and hides it under the couch. Drinking is for gangsters and tsotsis with no morals, for those who abandon their families and waste all their money on themselves. She does not drink. She is not this person.

. . .

Gary can't sleep. He rolls away from Mike to shield him from the light of his cellphone and checks Twitter, again. #MandelaDay is trending already. Is that a good thing? People are interested, at least. Gary and his team will be "part of the conversation" this year, just as he promised his boss—his boss who is somehow skeptical of social media even though he's only thirty-eight. Today is a small sideline thing, barely a drop in the marketing budget, but Gary argued so hard for it and now his idealism feels heavy. Every other bright-eyed millennial brand manager in the country is doing the same thing. How will his good deed be any different?

He extricates himself from Mike and the duvet and makes his way to the kitchen. It's about emotional engagement, he reminds himself as he puts on the kettle, not exposure. Their customers will love that they're giving back. Even if they don't tell their friends about it, they'll become more loyal to the brand. He stares at the sea for a while. It's the same dark grey as the granite countertops, as the sky. The kettle flicks off, losing its blue glow as the water comes to rest. He's overthinking the whole thing.

Gary takes his coffee to the living room and fires up his laptop. Bronwyn and Chantelle have sent him photos of them loading paints and rollers and t-shirts into Bron's car last night. They're standing on either side of the open trunk with manic grins and raised thumbs. It's a great pic. Gary tweets it from the brand account and uploads it to the blog he set up for today.

Mike stumbles in, wiping sleep from his eyes. "Thank God it stopped raining, hey? Would have made your kumbaya save the world day a mess."

"Didn't you have a meeting to get to?"

Mike grins and kisses Gary on the cheek. He's infuriatingly pleased with himself. "I'm playing, baby. You're a legend for making it happen. Can I make you some eggs?"

. . .

There's not much jam left in the tin, so Nombulelo spreads it thin. She has enough bread for five sandwiches. She packs them into a plastic bag and heads for the taxi rank. She can't face the walk to school today.

Everyone with a job and a place to be is standing in line in the early morning fog. It's the busiest time of day, draining the township into the city. This was Nombulelo's life every day until a few months ago when the family she cleaned for moved to Australia. They said they'd find her another job but her age must have counted against her. No one wanted a cleaner who took all morning just to vacuum the house.

A young man shifts to make room for her in a taxi and she thanks him but there's music in his headphones and it's so loud no one can hear her speak. Beside him, a woman sits with a small girl on her lap, hiding and revealing herself from behind her hands to squeals of delight. Nombulelo fixes her eyes on the road ahead. When the driver's music comes on it's a relief. It rattles the windows and shakes her chest. No small talk, no giggles from the child, no thoughts.

"Thirteen, Gogo," shouts the collector over the din.

"I'm only going down the road."

"Fine. Give me three."

She takes out her wallet and remembers, before she opens it, that there is nothing inside. She holds the wallet in her lap and pretends to count out change as warmth spreads from her neck into her cheeks. The other passengers pass their fare forward. The conductor makes change and passes it back. Perhaps she will be overlooked.

"It's three rand, Gogo" he says again. He is wearing sunglasses even though the sun is lost behind cloud.

"Can I give you a sandwich?" she says at last.

The driver pulls onto the side of the road and stops. "Get out," he says. She is barely out of the taxi before the other passengers start gossiping. The young man takes his headphones off and shouts something, but she is not going to listen. Doesn't he have anything better to do? He doesn't know her life. Nobody knows her life but they all have opinions about it. She should go back to church. She should talk to people. She should try to move on. Ma'Khumalo even told her not to spend all her money on city doctors for Thembi. "They do the same thing as the nurses at the clinic" she said, as if she knew what she was talking about, as if the nurses at the clinic hadn't given Thembi aspirin tablets and sent her home. Aspirin tablets!

The man with the headphones stops her. He has paid the conductor and offers her a twenty rand note, which he won't take back. She is too tired to fight. "God bless you," she says. He smiles at her with surprising warmth. "We have to make our own blessings, Gogo."

Shacks and clotheslines fly past the window, and rows of concrete outhouses and skinny dogs in the gaps between them and nothing ever changes. Even the people look the same as when Nombulelo moved here, though they can't be the same because she's grown old in that time.

She gets out at the small compound of tooth-colored buildings just short of the freeway. Boys kick a soccer ball around in the yard of one of the new housing projects that flank the freeway. She promised Thembi they would live in one of those developments, with running water and brick walls like white people. "We'll be kings!" Thembi had said, thrusting her tiger into the air. "You can be the main king, granny, but I also get to be one."

Nombulelo hands sandwiches out at the school gates. No one will take them.

"We have lunch today, Gogo" says one of the girls.

"They brought us food" says another, gesturing to the group of people unpacking the paints.

A third girl takes out some change and offers it to Nombulelo. It's Ma'Khumalo's granddaughter. Ma'Khumalo must have told her to take pity on Nombulelo.

"I don't want your money," she says. She will not get angry. Not today. They are painting the tiger for Thembi. A small piece of her will live on.

"Are you okay, Gogo?" the girl says. Nombulelo puts a hand on her shoulder and waits for the dizziness to pass. It's punishment for last night, she knows, but she can't get dizzy today. She excuses herself and makes her way to the bathrooms in Block C. She closes the cubicle door and takes out a small bottle from her skirt. The first sip singes her tongue, her throat, her stomach. The second sip is gentler. She sits for a moment on the closed toilet seat and breathes. The third sip is warm and forgiving. It soothes the tremors in her hands. A benediction for her tired heart.

. . .

It's great to see another housing project go up. This has three story units, angular lines and earthy tones of orange and brown—a distinctly African aesthetic. Gary's always telling Mike architects should do more stuff like this, be proud of where they're from. Mike's firm designs houses that look like they're from Scandinavian magazines—all planes of glass and textured wood. What relevance does that have? Gary checks the sign but can't find the architect credit.

He reads *This City Works For You* then he has to make the turn. He exits the freeway and makes sure his doors are locked.

At the school, Bronwyn and Chantelle are distributing t-shirts—green and white to match the brand colors. Gary snaps a few pics of the kids pulling them on, then wanders around the classrooms taking before-shots. The walls are cracked and peeling and filthy. A great contrast for the blog. "We'd like to give a warm welcome to our sponsors and thank them from the bottom of our hearts," the headmaster says when Gary gets back to the quad. "We know there are many communities in need and we appreciate that you chose to work with us." The students cheer and clap and Gary gets a great shot of some of the younger students raising their hands in the air like they're at church.

When Gary first called the headmaster he said he wanted to do something playful for the young kids. They agreed all the buildings would be green and white to keep Gary's boss happy, but the nursery school block would get a giant mural of a jungle. The jungle's already been sketched on the wall and it looks fantastic. Childlike and na-ive but not too simplistic or ugly. Properly authentic.

Gary sets up his laptop in one of the classrooms. The kids outside start singing Rihanna and he hears Chantelle and Brad and Siya join in. He leans back against the wall and tries to live in the moment, to be truly present for this. No fussing over social media analytics and the perfect headline. This is what makes it all worth doing.

When he gets outside there's an old woman painting with the kids. She's not wearing the t-shirt and she looks kind of homeless.

"Her granddaughter died," says the headmaster, reading his eyes. "She was in the nursery school so we thought it would be nice to include her. I'll ask her to leave."

"Don't do that," Gary says. She probably should be part of it. He finds it weird but that's a cultural chasm he's working on bridging. Life in the townships is messy.

"Smile!" he says, and snaps a few action shots.

"Hey you," he says at the old woman, "Can you smile please?"

She does not smile. She glares at him with eyes full of hatred. It's as if he's been punched in the chest. He goes for a walk to resuscitate his excitement. He videos some of the kids, applauds the completion of Block B. When he gets back to the nursery school the old woman is slopping orange paint all over the place.

"Everyone! Everyone! Stop for a second, please. Thanks. So our brand is about being Southern Africa experts so we've gotta make sure the picture is of African animals. Okay? We're in Africa, guys. Let's celebrate it!" His voice lets him down, making him sound like every patronizing old white guy he grew up hating. God this is awful. "Lions, giraffes, rhinos," he continues, "no tigers, okay?"

The old woman shouts something but the students distract her. "I'm so sorry, Gary," the headmaster says, "I didn't think! Of course, we all know your tagline. I should have thought. We'll make it a lion. Let's give this jungle a king!"

The painting resumes and the woman slops more orange paint against the wall.

She sways from side to side. A student near her tries to take her brush away but she won't let it go. She pushes him against the wall and gets paint all over his t-shirt. Why does there have to be a scene, for fuck's sake? Is it such a big deal to paint a fucking lion?

The headmaster whispers something in her ear and she screams "I will not!" His eyes are wide with panic or embarrassment or both. She starts to sing. It sounds like a hymn but she's forgotten all the words. She's clearly drunk. The headmaster reaches for her shoulder but she shakes him off, stumbles backwards and falls onto the ground, sending mini brandy bottles tumbling out of her skirt and knocking over a tin of paint which spills all over her legs and feet. He lifts her by the armpits and drags her to the gates. She fights and shouts and the older children try not to watch.

Once locked out, the woman sings from the side of the road. Gary can't make sense of the words through her drunken slurring but her voice is almost beautiful. It soars and retreats, masterful and impassioned and dignified, like it's forgotten to whom it belongs, like she is not this crumpled, broken woman.

"I hope this isn't all you take from to-day," the headmaster says, "and you come back again in the future." Gary smiles at him and tries to remember why he's here. The kids get a new school, he'd said to Mike. The marketing team gets to do something meaningful. He picks up a paint brush and helps with the baobab tree. The lion starts to take shape. The woman's singing gets softer and stops. She gets up off the ground and shuffles down the street, leaving a lop-sided trail of orange paint in the dirt.

Gary checks the ground for any mini brandy bottles that fell from her skirt, but someone has tidied them away already. Those don't need to be in the pictures.

1,098 LIKES

BODY
MEMORY

Creative Nonfiction

Illustrated by Kim Herbst
Written by Michelle Spokes

when we were at a fetish party watching the man who used to be your dom demonstrating how to snap a whip, you pulled me onto your lap—as a statement. your arms wrapped around my ribs so tightly i could only take shallow breaths. my heart beat. my pussy pulsed. you held me there, making your claim, until we left mid demo, your hand holding mine.

the first time we held hands in public, walking across a parking lot, i hoped someone i knew drove by and saw us.

your finger stroking from the bridge of my nose to the tip and back up again, a trick to help me fall asleep. worked every time.

the backs of your thighs resting on the fronts of mine when i spooned you and the tops of your thighs tucked behind mine when you spooned me.

the smack of your hand, the red welt shape of it on my ass. the circular warmth of your palm smoothing away the sting.

your eyes looking into my eyes. my eyes deferring, looking down. my eyes diverting to your mouth. your mouth directing vibrations of gratitude and devotion into the canals of my ears. the buzz of your words moving in tune with my myocardium.

when your mouth overlapped mine and your tongue exchanged the taste of cheap wine with mine.

when the sweet smoke in your throat exited your lips and rose to the roof of my mouth then settled in my lungs. because i declined a hit, you became a bong.

your tough, mischievous, uneven smile. your mouth opening as you laugh. my palm cupping your shoulder, your elbow. us with our jokes snapping like rubber bands, talking at the same time and still understanding each other's fast minds.

the mascara wand between your thumb and forefinger, gently tugging my eyelashes. when you exhale, your breath soft on my face. the playful swish of the blush brush over my cheekbones. you saying, 'now look at me,' and biting your lip as you assess.

the day you decided it was time to instruct me. handing me the mascara. demonstrating. taking turns with me in the mirror, in a tiny public bathroom, laughing.

my foot on the carpet and the little brush between your fingers painting my toenails red.

every week, new colors on your nails, even yellow one time, one time blue, seasonal colors for holidays. rainbow for a trip to cherry grove. the pad of my index finger tapping the new color scheme to acknowledge. smooth nail polish or a slight texture to an overlay of sparkles.

your skin smooth as satin, as baby powder, against any part of my body. you slather lotion on after every shower, free samples lifted from where you work. there are boxes you've given me, tiny bottles of aveeno, cerave, neutrogena and so on in my linen closet. i've made the post-shower routine a habit, too, but my skin isn't as silky.

your arm through the crook of mine; my stride awkward, syncopated, trying to match your natural rhythm, swagger and sway.

the hum and purr in my elbow when my phone's on the desk at work and a text comes through. the thrill in my veins when i see your name on the screen. every time. my thumbs tapping letters, punctuation marks, spelling out our own version of shorthand, scrolling for bitmojis, and gifs, racing with yours. messages whisking through intangible space like dragonflies on certain summer days.

flannel sheet under us, portable speaker playing "no place i'd rather be,' a jones beach bass boom behind that, my head on your lap. my face looking up at the underside of your chin, at the blue blue sky. you leaning forward and me in the perfect spot for that.

your tongue sucking tequila from my belly button.

while you drive, your right hand on my inner thigh.

all the times you've headed south, and peeked north from between my knees.

the vacuum in my stomach when i need to hear from you and don't.

the birthday you wanted to be alone and didn't even want me to visit, and i drove to your rented room anyway and wiped your snot with my sleeve, pulled you close, kissed you all over your face, and your tears wet my lips, and your lips were puffy against mine.

when the hinge of my hips balanced on your windowsill, hands bracing forward motion, feet out in the night. you'd called repeatedly and told devastating secrets in a strange voice, then hung up. i found you asleep. you woke up groggy from sleeping pills that shouldn't have mixed with your meds. the next day you denied calling. the list of recent calls on your phone proved you did.

the time you arrived at my house on a cold

winter night as i finished a shower. each of your hands landing on each of my breasts, so pink from the hot water. a reversal, since i'm the one with cold hands and yours are small furnaces. somehow these lyrics spin into that moment: 'story of my life… i drive all night… i spend her love, until she's broke, inside.'

my body hiccupping with sobs and your voice. my body seizing with orgasm and your voice. my denials, my confessions, my stories and your ears, your interruptions, your questions.

my temple against your shoulder blade as we sleep.

. . .

some months after you found your man, i sat on a rocking chair watching you on top. i fixated on his pale, narrow, nervous feet and how they didn't move.

when you and i lay down on your bed, equal- ly ready, our eyes, lips and legs locked. we intensified. he left the room.

when a flattened silence lay in my throat
the whole week you two were gone on the
road trip. you met his family, envisioned life
there instead of here, and began planning
for that. the hollow crackle of those summer nights.

your flattery, his happy blush, my lungs fill-
ing with air.

the other night, my own man hit a spot
inside that hurt, that your knuckle, when
you'd wriggled your fist into me, had also
hurt, and in a burst of pain, quick as strobe
lights, i was with you, then back with him.

at your place, content, present, snuggled
next to you on the couch, my cheek against
your swollen breast and my forearm resting
across your round belly.

in my backyard, springtime sun on our faces. my daughter talking to your belly button, introducing herself.
at my house, your hips between my knees.
the heels of my hands massaging your
back. this body of yours, wider now, speaks

of change. we already know how to work around a baby's life, finding time for just us. already know how to walk beside a child, each of us holding a hand, counting to three, then swinging the light body up into her own laughter. already, we can imagine my daughter holding your newborn in her arms. not sisters, but just about, for a little while.

your back to me as you sleep in your bed. my arm slung around the width of you, my hand wide on the warm, taut skin. i feel movement. my eyes brim. the motion, however, is rhythmic. it isn't the baby. it's the effort of your breathing. a week from now, your hand will tug mine, press it low against your belly, and there, a hello, swift as a fish, will find my palm. in the meantime, my forehead finds a resting spot against your shoulder blade for the night.

for a time we will have a brief island of balance before you leave what has been us, to reside further than a day's drive away from me, and slip out of reach, maybe fall out of touch.

THE BALLOON LOAN

Fiction

Illustrated by Plum
Written by Emily Zasada

It was mid-December and the dealership was shimmering both outside and in when Jimmy brought them to me late in the day. Handed me their folder and shot me that look he always does, the one that means Please. He's as dumb as a lug wrench and believes he can squeeze a deal out of a rock. Which, as a matter of fact, he has done—a number of times—but only with my help.

I flashed him my usual grin—I've got this, Jimmy. But it wasn't until he'd left and I pointed them to their chairs, and I saw the curve of her stomach as she turned to sit that I understood what I was dealing with.

Just for a moment, I hesitated. Outside my locked glass door, I could see them still swirling around, the dreamers and the idiots. Money trembles at the top of their bank accounts like beer foam, just waiting to spill out. You can see it, how the wanting sweeps through them like a fever. You can see it in their eyes.

It was in their eyes, too. The eyes of the couple on the other side of my desk.

"We want a low payment," the man said. He sounded rough, like he'd been chewing on shot glasses.

As soon as she thought I wasn't looking, his wife shot him a look. Ah, so: she's the smarter one, I thought. Always good to identify that one up front, from my perspective. But still: from the model of the car that Jimmy had written on their folder, neither one of them was very smart. Their credit was up on the screen in front of me, and it told a story of impulse and greed. One or both of them needed comfort, often and desperately, and they liked it delivered in the form of things they could attach their fevered desires to, and climb in.

The wife moved forward in her chair. "Do you know-" she began to ask. Then she lifted up a hand. A small wedding ring glittered in the light. I don't know why but I quickly covered up my own with my other hand, like I was ashamed of it or something. Everyone is a different person in a different situation, I guess, and in that room I wanted to show her that I was what a strong independent woman could be. That it was still time for her to get out and make her own choices, even with that little bump under that thin blue top she was wearing. Still, I don't know why I would care. It's my choice to wear it to the dealership every day, even though I've been going home alone to a little apartment for years where my only company is my cats. It's my lie to tell.

"Oh—" The hand fell back down. "Never mind. I guess you're not the person to ask."

"What?" The husband shifted in his chair. It was obvious: he'd never worked at a desk and probably never would. He hated being there, but it was a sacrifice he'd chosen to make to whatever gods he believed would move into his body when he took hold of the car keys and make him one of them. "You aren't going on and on about that safety report you read again, are you? Listen, Lils, we're getting that car. Look where we are. It's almost done."

I was desperate to move the conversation along to finance rates. Because no one knew better than me that no car was truly safe. People want to believe that they can make themselves safe, but they can't. We're all made out of the flimsiest materials. Little packages of blood and bone that can be pierced at any moment.

I asked them if they were interested in leasing or financing, and how long they were planning on keeping the car. In their eyes you could see the future spinning out in a way that was new for them. She was thinking five years down the line, I guessed, trying to picture this baby who was still a stranger drinking juice in the back seat. Watching her with eyes that reminded her of herself, or him, or both. And he was wondering if he would still even be with her. If she would even matter anymore.

I could tell: They didn't know what they wanted. They had no idea.

"You don't know what you want, Tessa," was one of the final things he said to me. We were in that sad kitchen in our old apartment. Sticky stains on the cabinets that wouldn't come off, and the counter littered with empty beer cans and wine bottles for recycling. The thing about it is that he was right. I had no idea what I'd wanted. After what happened, I'd tried religion for a while before I'd turned to drinking, but neither did much of anything. And the affair, too, with the Indian car salesman who wore that beautiful steel bracelet, like cold clouds on a

windy day. That didn't work either. Not that he ever knew about that.

It was maybe two weeks before the papers were signed and he was gone for good. Ben had been dead for two years.

"Just see what you can do with the payment," the man said again. He twisted his body away from the woman's, as if he were sending her a message, or himself. "I'm not committing until I have a number."

They were young, but old enough to have made mistakes. Most of the numbers I could give them were swollen from their past choices.

All except for the balloon loan.

The final payment would hit them when love staggered away under the weight of the bills and the arguments and the stress. When their child was no longer a wee bean that gurgled at the world with wonder, and was instead a real, tiny person who could say *I want.* When they passed one another in their hallway at night and averted their eyes to avoid seeing one another's ordinariness.

That was when the final payment would hit. That was when the bill would be due.

Outside the glass pane of the door, Jimmy paused, waiting to catch my eye. His face shining with hope. Past him the windows glittered with the reflections of everyone hunting down the last deals of the day.

Here, all of them believed in me. Here, I was a god in a tiny world.

I thought again of what he said to me, my ex. How I didn't know what I wanted. *Oh, I do know what I want, you bastard,* I thought as I printed out their paperwork for the balloon loan. The empty dreams in the dealership surged around me like a song. Nothing here matters, but all of it is as real as anything else. Florescent lights beamed down on my kingdom as I pulled the papers off the printer. *It's this,* I thought, as I placed the papers in front of them to sign. *I want this.*

WHEN THE RAINS COME

Fiction

Illustrated by Renata Srpcanska
Written by Tee Indawongse

Nahm wipes the sweat from her brow with the hem of her shirt, sees the black city smog stain the cloth. It is hot here in the city, where the days are long and the nights are short and the city is never dark. Lights are strung up from post to post, leaving behind thick black trails of exposed wires like modern vines. Her reed-woven shoes slap against the uneven cobblestones as she walks. Mosquitoes hover, lazy, as if the summer air is too humid even for them.

There are the war machines rolling down the street in all their military glory, wreathed in jasmine and marigold garlands. They are affectionately known as war elephants, because underneath all the glamour the bulky tanks are gunmetal grey. They belch out plumes of black smoke into the already polluted air. Despite their decorations, they are colossal beasts made of pistons and steel, lumbering about the narrow streets, and yet there are still vendors who walk fearlessly beside them, calling out their wares. The closest woman to Nahm is selling fried banana chips by the bagful; it smells delicious, and reminds her of her hunger.

She cannot stop to eat yet. She has one more house to go. It's quite possibly her least favourite. The house is a distance away from her usual route, but consistently pays well enough to compensate. The high brick fence is topped with glued down shards of broken glass in shades of bottle-blue-green. The poor man's barbed wire. Feral dogs patrol the area, and it stinks of piss and dirt. There is a spirit house outside, but it is unkempt, uncared for, and it makes Nahm wince to see it. Perhaps it is not quite so fashionable to follow the old ways, but you don't need to believe to respect.

Nahm is let in by one of the servants—Fah, who Nahm likes most of the household. When you see Fah, you understand why she's called that. She's all sharp angles and bone, birdlike with a hooked nose and dark eyes. She looks a second away from taking off into the sky, always braced on the tips of her toes, like gravity isn't strong enough to hold her.

"Thank you for coming," Fah says, with a bit of a Southerner's accent. Her manners are impeccable as always, and as usual, Nahm tries to think of a way of extending the hand of friendship past the barrier of civility. "Sir is in his room."

Like most of the houses in the city, it's several storeys high. After removing her shoes, Nahm makes the familiar trek up the narrow flights of stairs, the tiled floors a cold contrast against her feet. She notes the familiar dark shadows of unlit rooms; its perfect neatness, its empty spaces. It's quiet here, almost unbearably so, and she wishes for the cacophony of outside to invade this still, unwelcoming place.

The door is open, and she knows she does not need to knock. She steps inside to see the silhouette of a man sitting by the window. He is a gnarled figure, bent with age and bitterness. Despite the painful-looking hunch of his shoulders, he is kinetic in tiny bursts; the erratic twitch of his fingers and the impatient tap-tap-tap of his feet.

"Little *kratāy*," he says, and Nahm reluctantly moves forward. He is the only one who can call her that. Little rabbit, he says, for the rabbit you can see on the moon when it's full and the night is clear. He always says it as if affectionate, as if he isn't poking fun at her round face and overlarge front teeth.

He's always been cruel, and all the crueller for smiling as he bites down into you.

"Hello, uncle," she says, polite and soft. They share no blood, but he has insisted on her calling him that since the beginning. "How are you today?"

A noise of disgust escapes him. "If I were well, would I be seeing you?"

Nahm thinks of monsoons, thinks of its wrath, and thinks of the crash of waves against a pebble beach. She takes a deep breath, trying to sweep away the violent energy within her. "Of course, uncle. Would you like me to begin?"

After a jerky nod of consent, Nahm pulls out her little kit filled with tools and other miscellany. Uncle snorts, disgruntled, before shifting to lift the hem of his shirt to reveal a metal chest plate, which is dented and ill-kept, littered with scratch-marks and spots of rust.

This, in its own way, is just another conquered land in the name of war.

Nahm settles down and begins her duties. She does surgeon's work even as her hands dirty with grease. She knows that a heart must sit several inches from her fingers, but even with proximity, Nahm can't think of how cold, shrivelled uncle could have one inside him.

"What are you doing, little *kratāy*?" he asks.

"Fixing you, uncle," Nahm replies. His chest plate is cold, and her fingers are slowly going numb.

. . .

The city glitters, metal-bright, under the sun that sits too close in the heavens. Any closer and perhaps people would burn where they stand. The air is so humid you could very nearly open your mouth to take a drink of it; so hot that if you look in the right spots, reality shimmers.

Lately there has been an influx of *farang* in the streets; fair-haired foreigners walking the streets with one hand on their weapons. Perhaps war had been swapped out with peace for the sake of trade agreements, but the peace is still tenuous at best. An unpeace, an unwar—a truce of hidden daggers.

Nahm is walking through tight space between stalls in a bustling marketplace. If Krung Thep is the heart of Siam, then she

is running along one of its many name-
less veins. She keeps an eye out for sticky
fingers, protective of the money so recently earned. These alleys are a pickpocket's
dream; a crushing mess of humanity, a press
of skin to skin every few steps. She prefers
to give this place a wide berth, but she is on
the search for replacement parts.

The rich, perhaps, could afford new
mechana parts, but Nahm works with
the working class. Like with clothes and
shoes and handbags—this marketplace is
where the best knock-offs and second-hand
mechana wares are to be found.

"*Kah, kah,*" the seller says, placating.
She's a young girl, only a few years older
than Nahm by the looks of it, but already
running the front of shop by herself. The
place is rusting and old, more grime on the
walls than paint. "Only 1800 *baht* then?"

Nahm stands firm and manages to hag-
gle down to 1650. She's been in the business
long enough to know the weight and feel of
quality, and what that's worth. Honestly,
1650 *baht* is already more than she would
usually pay, but there's been a slow-down in
production, and fewer pieces are entering

the market. Basic supply-demand. Nahm barely can read her letters, never finished school, but that she knows well enough.

She spends another thirty *baht* on a light lunch for herself, thin noodles in cloudy broth, with few dumplings and a handful of steamed vegetables for colour. It's late in the day for lunch, and there are few others eating. The shop is barely that, a noodle stand based in the small space from the overhang of a building, a literal hole-in-the-wall, with rickety mismatched chairs and three tables total that wobble from the cracks in the concrete. It faces out to a small side street, so closely that if Nahm were to reach out, her fingers could brush against those who rode past on bikes.

The cook takes a break from the noodle stand, wiping his hands with his apron. He goes around cleaning bowls left behind, straightening condiment stands, and picking up a left-behind newspaper.

"I don't like the look of them," Nahm says, gesturing at the cover with her chopsticks.

The cook grunts in agreement, looking at the paper with a grimace.

A grainy picture of a *reubiin* looks up at them from yesterday's paper. It is hard to make out the details, but the size of the things can't be denied. It looks like one would take up the length of several rice fields. There's been a lot of talk following the king saying that these airships are going to be the next step for Siam's future. All Nahm can think is, *how can they fly?*

She thinks of the delicate flutter of hearts as she tinkers, her clever hands and nimble fingers. She thinks of how she spends her days fixing those who are broken from bombs and artillery shells. Nahm thinks of swooping birds of prey, of hunters looking for blood. Unbidden, she thinks of bird-like Fah, of her falling, of whether it's possible to fix broken wings.

. . .

After handing over her blood money to the local police station—a quarter of her earnings to ensure they look the other way to a poor girl working without a licence or the appropriate paperwork—Nahm has enough money to send some home this month. Not much, but every little bit helps.

Her mother sent her to the city years ago with dreams of getting a doctor or a teacher for a child, have Nahm do something respectable with her life. At least, that's what she always said. Privately, of late, Nahm thinks the decision was more to do with the fact there were six other children under that roof and none of them had quite the temper Nahm had.

Born in a monsoon, under a full moon, in a village that redefined the colour green with every harvest—her mother always said to her she had all the violence of water, but needed to channel its serenity. Nahm tries to think of a gentle creek, but more often than not feels like a river overflowing, rushing and unstoppable.

So to Krung Thep she was sent. Alone and with a heavy weight on her shoulders. She was to learn and make her family proud. Then the war broke out, and Nahm had no mind for books and no patience for teaching, but she was good with her hands. Where war went, the wounded followed in its wake, and Nahm finds steady work in the repair of people left behind.

There are worse things to bear, Nahm

thinks. There may not be a great deal of honour in the work she does, nor a great deal of accolades, but her family accept her money when she sends it, and that's enough for now.

. . .

There is another military parade today, one of many celebrations for the upcoming New Year. They seem to happen more often than not, these days. War elephants are trundling down the streets, the life of the city momentarily halted to allow for their movement through. Nahm stops on her way to uncle's house to watch the spectacle. Her eyes slide over the decorations and the marching soldiers. She watches the crowd, and a heavy weight of discomfort settles in her gut. Something is wrong.

A siren cuts through the bustle of everything, sharp and shrill. Instinctively, everyone looks to the sky. They're clear blue, empty, and suddenly so viciously threatening. Nahm has her eyes still on the crowd, and she realises: all the heads are black-haired. Where did all the fair-haired *farang* go?

Evacuate, a loudspeaker says. *Evacuate. Evacuate.*

She is pushed like a leaf downstream as the tides of people around her rush towards the nearest shelter. It has been years since they have been needed, but their doors open without protest, and the space inside is well kept. As if waiting, knowing.

Shelters are all based underground, with low ceilings and harsh orange lights. Some of the bulbs have been burned out, so there are patches of disquieting dark. The walls are bare brick, gritty to touch. The air smells stale at first, then transforming to the pungent tang of sweat and fear.

Nahm feels distress creeping up her throat like bile. She forces her way to the edge of the room, presses her hand against the wall and tries to hold steady against the flow. Faces pass her by in a blur, some familiar, most not.

One, very familiar.

"Fah," she gasps, grabbing an arm without thinking.

Fah stops and turns around. She smiles politely at Nahm and moves smoothly to join her against the wall and out of the flow of increasingly panicked people.

"Hello, Nahm," she says, calm. "It is good to see you are safe."

"As safe as you are, I guess," Nahm says.

"Where is uncle?"

"Sir preferred to stay at home."

"Stubborn old man."

"I agree," Fah says, unexpectedly wry.

A moment of silence falls. It ripples out, almost, a hush descending like a blanket over the room. Before, sirens meant falling bombs. It meant destroyed buildings, it meant people dying. To Nahm, it meant more work. More mechana to buy, to insert, to adjust. She feels dizzy though, looks around and sees people crying, stifled sobbing, people praying.

The loudspeakers have switched messages. A voice is repeating, *The king will keep Siam safe. Our reubiin will keep our skies safe. There is no war we cannot win.*

"Do you believe that?" Nahm asks, lips barely moving, the question riding on the shallowest of breaths. Questioning the king can be tantamount to treason around the right ears.

Fah leans back against the wall, sighing. Her reply is just as quiet. "We have the land and the sea. If we get the sky, then perhaps."

"Who is to say the *farang* will not get the land and sea?"

A small smile turns the corners of Fah's mouth. "Only faith."

Together, they wait out the rest of the sirens. When the loudspeakers fall silent, they sleep through the night in the first true darkness Krung Thep has seen for years. If they were outside, Nahm would guess she might even be able to see the stars coming out for the New Year.

In Siam, you mark the New Year with a giant water fight. You throw water on your friends, your loved ones, strangers on the street. It means a fresh start and a clean slate. Nahm dreams of monsoons, of the city raining with not a cloud in the sky, and she dreams of flying.

QUEEN OF WINGS

Fiction

Illustrated by Plum
Written by Michael Lehman

One time there was a girl living way out in the woods with her father in a cabin all alone. I know her name, but I ain't gonna tell it to you, 'cause I hear she's still on the run.

Her father was tall and thin. Stringy, you might say. He got that way from eating pieces of string like they was noodles with sauce on top and everything, and string beans, and nothing else. But out in the woods the girl and him didn't have much of anything to eat. He was too proud to farm in the dirt and he was a lousy hunter. They would have starved except the wolves took pity on him and left out a few scraps of rotten meat.

He was too proud to chop wood or draw water or mend the roof or any of that, and so the girl did as much as she could. Fact was, he'd been a rich man, the owner of a whole coal mine back in the east. He couldn't hold on to it, though, on account of some of the miner's daughters he summoned to his mansion for "instruction" were never seen again, and the town, even though it was a company town, and even though it was his company, grew restless, and on some dark night in some dark room with the windows shut the word "justice" was even mentioned, and he took his own little daughter and lit out for the west before that justice got any more real.

So they lived in a cabin all alone in the woods, and the girl, despite her hunger, grew stronger. She would slip away from the cabin and lie among the hummocks of deep moss and intricate lichen and it was almost, as she slept and dreamed, almost like the mother she'd lost. And she listened to the birds and learned from them how much food there is to find in a forest.

When she'd reached a certain span, her father brought out a dress a miner's daughter had worn, a dress he'd folded and saved and carried all the way out to the woods, and he commanded the girl to put it on. Then he threw a great big pile of the wood she'd chopped on the fire and paced around and around the cabin floor reading aloud in a thunderous voice from the most boring part of the book of Leviticus and snapping a stockman's whip he happened to have among his possessions for no reason.

What would you do, if you were the girl? It's not such a simple question. He was her father, you know. The only life she had ever known. But you're right, in the end, she ran out the door. And do you know what else she did? She nailed the door shut from the outside and set fire to the cabin and watched it burn until she was sure her father was dead.

She walked away for days and nights without end, and came to the tracks, and climbed aboard a train going west. She figured she'd ride to end of the line, where natives patrolled the ramparts of the Sierra Nevada with good Chinese steel. The rumor she'd heard from the birds was that a refugee might be allowed to cross the frontier.
In California they gambled with yarrow stalks and the prizes were the past and future. She wanted to live in a country where everything was strange. It would be like dunking her head in a bucket of cool, clean water.

She climbed aboard the saloon car. There was a man in the corner with huge side whiskers and blue tinted glasses playing a jangling little piano that rattled with the rails. There was a bartender with a mous-

tache like a whisk broom slouched on the bar and a bunch of gamblers in black Stetson hats around a table playing cards.

"Sit down and mix some biscuits with these boys," one of the gamblers said.

She sat down at the table and laid her father's money down. They dealt her in. She looked at her cards. The suits were sails, wings, wheels, and hooves. A wasp lit on her ear. When the gamblers saw it, they shouted, they reached towards her face, they did all the things that would make it sting. She held up her hand to still them. It was not a gesture they would ordinarily have respected from a girl. But at that moment it seemed to come through the train wheels from the silence deep under the earth. The wasp crawled into the little amphitheater of the inner ring of her ear and buzzed and buzzed. The buzzing unraveled seams in space and time and she saw herself, and the gamblers, sitting at different tables, playing other cards, reflected back into infinity like mirrors facing each other. They sat in a mud hut beside a road paved with stones. Her face was lined with tattoos. The suits were coins, whips, seeds, and graves. She stood under the open sky and the gamblers were wolves all around her. She held a burning ball of pitch wrapped in moss in her hands.

She turned in one card and drew The Wanderer.

"That ain't even s'posed to be in this deck," said one of the gamblers.

"That means we get all your money," said another.

"It means I go free at the border," she said.

"Now miss . . ." said a gambler. "What's all this talk about 'going free?' What does that even mean?"

She raised the butt of her father's pistol just a hair to where it caught the light and they could she had them all covered under the table.

"I'd tell you," she said. "If I thought it would do any good."

CHRYSALIS

Fiction

Illustrated by Sophie Page
Written by Sarah Tinsley

The doctor placed her on the scales—a wriggling apple weight.

"60th percentile."

One hand pressed on the frog-bent legs, held them against the scale. Iris willed the little thing to lift its pudgy head, find a neck underneath those squashy folds to stretch out.

"45th." That sounded accusing.

"She's still on breast milk. And the baby-led weaning, I hate the way it makes her cough, but-" the words caught in her throat. "We watch Baby University, and play games." What wasn't she doing?

"Tablet?" He scrolled down a list.

"No." She hated to see small eyes fixed on those flickering squares. "We play with toys, and balls. She has a lot of books. We wriggle on the floor every day." That was her favourite time. Lying back and squirming under rainbow-tangled lights from the crystals in the window.

"Tablet computers provide the most stimulation for the cost." Notes on the chart. Perhaps they had a found a reason for it, after all.

"I thought it was bad for their eyes." Something between pity and disappointment in the doctor's expression.

Lila was returned. Iris scooped her into the carrier around her waist. A trip to the shop then, for one of those awful electronic things.

Out on the street, parents, wary-eyed, cast glances at each other, scrutinised the tops of toddlers heads. Checking for the early signs. Autumn was the time to look out for it.

In other countries the season announced itself in a shout of colour. Here it was a reduced summer, as if someone had turned down the heat a notch, the plants withering. On the way home she passed the park. It used to be swings and slides, that bouncy space flooring in bright colours. All ripped out last year, when the first cases came to light.

At one end was the Interaction Section—bubble machines, drones to fly, crafts and building activities. The busiest was the Technology Zone—banks of screens where small fingers swiped and tapped, the odd shriek as a wailing victim was dragged off to be fed.

Next to the fence was Team Building. A group of toddlers huddled around their plinth. One girl in orange boots moved among them, sorting them into small groups and handing out materials.

Against Iris' chest, Lila had wilted into sleep. The warmth of that small mass seeped into clothing, a smell somewhere between sour and sweet. She couldn't help it. A quick peek under the hat—no scaly residue. Everything was fine.

Behind the fence, their structure grew. Tape and plastic, fuel cells tucked under in a wire mesh cage. Engagement was the key. The thing that would keep them.

When the marshall came over for testing, their balloon rocket exploded. The other one lifted on one corner and fell over, was declared the winner. In a flash of orange, the little girl was next to her culprit. The boy cowered, looking over to his parents for support behind the barrage of her attack.

The grown ups smiled. Iris saw nothing but desperation. She had to get away from all this stimulation. They used to say boredom was good for children.

Clusters of people made ragged shapes in the street. Long coats, boots, despite the temperature. International magazines painted a wash over all bodies. At home she could wear a T-shirt without ridicule in this heat. Avoid the looks she got as a lone parent. How could she possibly keep one, without help?

Back home, she made dinner. Cold blended soup and rice. Hot things made them warm and sleepy, encouraged hibernation. She put a couple of ice cubes in, for good measure. Next door they had their food delivered from Ice Times—lolly versions of kids food. Fish pops and Jelly ice.

Lila had always been quiet. They said it was a bad sign. Even at the birth. Awaiting a roar of life between her legs, Iris was alarmed to hear nothing at all, just her own gasping, the beep of the machines. The sound was supposed to make it official. A midwife plucked the pale skin. The baby had fallen asleep as soon as she came out.

Iris chatted over dinner, Lila's eating accompanied by a hum of pleasure. As soon as the food was off her face, Lila's eyes sagged. No time for a bath. Iris picked over the crown, looking for the sheen of something under the fine hair.

Once the cocoon of the blanket was over, the video monitor dangling overhead, it was possible to relax. At first, she hadn't been able to leave the room. Little by little, she moved the camp bed towards the door, finding a return to her bed was only possible when there was the grainy grey square of constant filming in her eyeline.

She flicked the telly on. Rates were up. 10% in Japan, 30% in Finland. Cities blamed the education system. There were crowds of women outside a school in China, thrusting games and snacks through the railings. Harder for them, to lose the only one they had.

Perhaps he was watching this. Wondering about the fate of his child. She'd not mentioned it, let him leave in his quiet way, edging out of her life by degrees. It was obvious in the circles under her eyes, the nausea over frying meat. If neither of them acknowledged it, they didn't have to discuss the possibility of tangling their futures together.

Outside, a sound. Like the moan of a siren. She peered into the street. Still light out, the wailing odd against the warmed orange sky.

It was Jackie, from over the road. The sound flickered out of an upstairs window, in between the flapping curtains. Another one.

Back in the bedroom, she fretted the blanket over Lila, pushing back the image of the brown husk that was smeared all over the newspapers. You couldn't get away from it. Yesterday, on the way back from the supermarket there'd been a woman handing out leaflets. Big picture of a leaf in the middle.

"Mother Earth is helping us."

She'd taken one, to avoid getting into conversation. It said it was nature's way of repopulating the world, making up for our mistakes. Easy to say if you didn't have any of your own.

Nigel, the boy that lived on the same road as Mum, he'd come out as a rhino. There was still a taped-over bit in the front door where he'd escaped, been picked up by the SRU to a more suitable location.

He'd been like that for weeks, apparently. Sheila had tried to hide him, soundproofed the door so the neighbours wouldn't hear him bellowing. Mum said he still liked his favourite food—Weetabix and honey—only in a bowl on the floor. The same eyes, Sheila said.

Iris crept back to the living room, the monitor clutched in her hand. It had to be a disease. Something in the genes, hidden until the crust started to form over the skin. Or a lack of love, of attention. All this nonsense about stimulation, it couldn't be good for them. Nothing more she could give there. Work had stopped calling, her weekly excuses withering away. There was money in the bank, it didn't matter. What use did tapping away at a screen do, now she had Lila? Everything had paled beside those piercing eyes.

After the news, a special report from Texas. A slight woman smiled out at the world. She cradled the cocoon in her arms—a blue-brown husk. She'd put a hat on it. Footage showed her pushing the thing around, strapped into the buggy.

"I've been chosen," she said. "Personally I hope she turns into a dolphin, so I got someone I can go for a swim with."

At the age of two Lila caught her sock on a nail. The scar was a red ribbon tied around her knee.

At three she found a shard of thrush egg in the park. It went into the box with the harlequin on, along with her other treasures—the stone from the seaside and a plastic Barbie shoe that had been discarded in a basket at Asda.

It wasn't long after her seventh birthday that Iris noticed it. Not on the scalp, as she'd expected, but a sheen on the bottom of her left foot. They were playing their usual game in the bath—Iris creating mounds of bubbles in the water that Lila flicked into the air with her toes, shrieking with pleasure. In the flurry of white, there was a thickening, just under the big toe.

She grabbed it, the reflexive muscles trying to pull away. It could be a scab, just a little hard patch. One finger stroked over it.

Smooth, almost metallic, a little cooler than the surrounding skin.

"It tickles!" Lila plopped her foot into the water, a large drop landing on Iris' cheek.

"You know I love you, right?" Iris stood up, the urge to play leaving her.

"More bubble towers." Lila leaned forward, scooping the remaining suds into rough mounds. Was that another patch on her back? Would the moles on her arm join up and seal her away?

"Bedtime." The tone of her voice jarred the little body, jumped it to attention, disappointment registering in the eyes. Iris bundled her into a towel, scrubbing the moisture away.

"Ow." It was said with deliberation.

"You're old enough to do this now." Iris pulled the plug and left the room, gripping her fingers against her palms. She wanted to hurt her. How dare she leave.

That was the first night the light was switched off without a story, no narrative to smooth the transition to sleep. Iris stayed up all night, clicking through the claims of cures, the parents who'd kept their children. Now the fault lay with affection, not stimulation. Millions had traded their tablets and computer consoles in for a Hug'Em, a contraption that allowed you to strap even a large child to your body, give them as much contact as possible. New articles about conversation cards to use with your toddler, groups of parents forming networks to help support single mothers and fathers, spreading their love thin to protect as many as possible.

National figures had decreased, she'd thought it was safe now. Seven was so old, so late, for the onset. When the birds announced the smudge of dawn in the sky, she crawled into Lila's bed, the hands clutching around her arm in sleep. It had been nothing, she would be fine in the morning.

It advanced quickly. By the following weekend there was a sheet of it on her back—hard, yet it rippled with the movement of her spine.

"How do you feel?"

"Fine. Can we go skating?" It was her new favourite pastime, now the summer had arrived. They put wheels on their feet and let gravity pull them down hills. Lila always pushed ahead, reaching the bottom before her mother. Iris gripped fences and lampposts, lessening her speed when she felt her feet pull away from her.

That night, after washing her hair, she massaged lotion into the brown patch. It slithered off, not changing in consistency at all.

"Does it hurt?" She felt for an edge, but there was nothing to get a nail under to peel it off.

"No." She was rearranging her crayons into colour order.

"How do you feel about it?"

"I don't know." The same answer, every time.

"You must feel something." She didn't want her to leave, couldn't imagine the shape of the hole that would be left behind.

"These things happen." A hand in hers, the large eyes serious, advanced in age. Arms around her neck, the scrawny body warm.

The following morning she pulled back the covers to a blue-brown pod. It was warm. Inside, things pulsed. It reminded her of

the peas they picked from Grandad's gar-
den, peeling back the green strings and
popping the little orbs in their mouths. Iris
sat, stroking her hand over the warm thing.
It wasn't as unpleasant as it looked on TV.
Somewhere between a banana skin and a
leaf. She spent the day lying next to it, whis-
pering the words she'd been saving for when
Lila was more grown up.

After a few days, it hardened. A dead
thing, a husk. She picked it up and took it
down to the living room. It was lighter than
she expected. Nothing to be seen beneath
the surface now, but she placed a blanket
over it just in case. Her days yawned open,
all those lumps of time empty. She found
herself talking to it, addressing the shape
as she made dinner, dusted, watched TV. All
her activities gravitated to the living room,
so she could be close to it.

Two weeks, that's what they said. Then
the new thing would come out, whatever
it was. Work hadn't asked, friends hadn't
called. Nothing could be said. As the time
approached she examined it closely, looking
for changes in shape, texture, colour, anything to give her a hint of the thing that

would emerge. Was that a hoof, tucked up in one corner? Perhaps the slight bulge near the top was a hump, or a pouch.

One morning, it started shaking. Very slight, the vibration only felt when she put her hand on it. Like a tiny heartbeat. It would not be long. She imagined the creature emerging, the Species Relocation Unit taking her daughter away in her new form. Was it still her? They hadn't been able to establish neurological similarity, because of the lack of communication possible.

She sat next to the quivering cocoon, flipping through photos on her phone. The harlequin box clasped between her hands, the bright white bandage against pink skin, the halo of hair, flung out as she whooshed down the hill by the park. This was her, not the thing she had become.

Placing the chrysalis on the back seat, she drove to the nearest hospital. There were flurries of sirens, the clatter of wheelchairs. Inside, through the swoosh of the door, rushing feet on hushed floors. She took the thing that used to be her daughter and placed it on a bench in the waiting area.

As she drove away, the wail of something

reached her through the open window. A cry she need no longer answer. Pulling into traffic, the city lights blinked, the moon an eye, watching her as she made her escape.

SEX WITH INDIANS

Fiction

Illustrated by Plum
Written by Chaya B.

We were working like sharks the winter I turned twenty-eight, when my ex-girlfriend got hired as my boss. The meeting where she made her introductions gave me pause. She'd been so harmless and androgynous and compact when we'd dated, but in the years since she'd gone from Gigi to her full name, Gloria Geetanjali, and grown into someone formal, and voluptuous and oblique.

Gigi was the one. She'd turned me onto girls to begin with. I'd picked her up somehow on a trip to Melbourne, where we met at a conference. This was long before I had learned how to pick up girls. There was a dinner, not far from the hostel where I was staying. I had no radar for these things, not then, but I was already turned on, not just by her but by how others were talking—Sid the beautiful Pakistani gay man with the calm white English professor boyfriend and the very confident suggestions on my hair; Marlene the viciously beautiful Mughal pale-skinned woman who ran some sort of lesbian charity and wanted to match-mate everyone—but never permanently—only until she honed in on the next victim, only to prove her theories about who wanted to taste who and how badly—and most important, Gigi née Gloria, a strange name for a Tamil girl, very wild Gloria, who kept fretting that I shouldn't get an arranged marriage, I just shouldn't. But I was wild about her instantly too, something convinced me that the way we were sitting, thigh to thigh, meant she would change the air I breathed that night, even though I'd sat that way a million times with a million different people, including attractive ones, and I'd never had much of a one-night stand, just four or five random hook-ups of impulsive near-nakedness that didn't go anywhere, not even to effective dry humping. I had wanted to be able to walk through the arranged marriage door, and was usually too nervous to start something that I knew my virginity couldn't last through.

Gigi was different though. She was an expert. The minute we got inside her place we kissed and kissed; soon she was on my hair and breasts with fingers and tongue and didn't stop until things happened to me, and we laughed because the end of my waist-length hair caught fire on the candle she'd been burning on her bed and without thinking I reacted, putting it out in a jiffy in her sink—then going back to her smooth gleaming body in the bed, and for that and for my quick learning she moaned and marveled: "You are amazing."

I was only twenty back then. The morning after, Sid said: "See how it worked not to pouf your hair out like that for no reason? Just let it be. Good things happen." (I didn't tell him about the fire.) Marlene said: "Yum. The two of you." But Gigi said: "You know I'll never settle down, don't you?"

It took me nearly a year to stop writing her romantic poetry. "Look, the main reason I had to sleep with you," she wrote me once, "besides that I just wanted to, so bad, was that I needed to stop you from getting an arranged marriage, darling. And look at you now. I saw the photo of that blonde girl you're dating. Mission accomplished. Mission fini. I saw the two of you kissing on the Institute website."

The Institute was where I'd been working since age twenty-one, an Institute "devoted to ending violence against women

and girls." In reality, it looked nothing like an Institute. It was a former bookie's office set above a fancy San Francisco Chinese restaurant. There weren't any signs on the door or anywhere. Grey, sparse, cluttered, it was inhabited by women working like sharks, quick, deadly and silent, seeking the weak spaces of the perps—then zeroing in efficiently, ravenous for justice, wielding restraining orders, guns, night sticks, self-defense classes, whatever it took to get the women out. To free our fellow creatures from cruel nets. Bite our way through. Intimidate if possible. Outsmart the enemy.

Gigi, Gloria, my Glo. Her mother had MS. Soon after we broke up, Gigi started calling me. On the worst days, we talked on the phone all night, often with extravagant silences—with Gigi still in Melbourne, me in San Francisco—paying by the minute just to hear each other breathe. In between tales of some white boy she was sort of crushing on but not really, she inserted descriptions of how her mom was going blind. Of how guilty her mother made her feel, deliberately. "Oh, listen to those birds singing. Soon I won't be able to see them.

I'll just have to listen. You'll have left me by then of course. Gone to America, I s'pose." Sigh. Gigi got job offers in the US on both coasts, but did nothing but wait. The year stable remission came, her mother regained most of her sight. Her mother started walking the Capital City Trail again, though with a walker, seeing through special lenses, refusing when Gigi offered to come along. Her mother even braved the safe parts of Great Ocean Road. Gigi's local friends (the ones she hadn't confided in, about her mother being sick) must have said: "Babe, you're so into those American surfer girls, you have to go."

G couldn't cure her mother by staying. She irritated the fierce resilient crone by hovering too much. My Gigi rationalized: "I'll make more money over there, then send it home," but then her mother surprised her and turned out to be thriftier than Gigi ever dreamed. "Three million saved for retirement, that's what I've got. I'm going to buy a boat while I'm alive," she decided.

So, Gigi took this job here in San Francisco, as my boss, without even telling me, not knowing for sure, even, that I was still at the Institute, and came in just as we were searching the ocean and the skies and the mountains and the land for bleeding girls, for the men who'd wounded them. For peace. There was no abiding justice, without peace—something me and Gigi both believed, but thought we'd never have.

There were meetings at the Institute. There were love triangles and not-love triangles—triangles for power alone, where women competed just for the pleasure of being looked at carefully. Especially among any new young girl and two older women, vying for the younger one's attention, time, favor, but above all—the power of provoking her anxiety. I always hated watching it. The way young women would storm in, flushed and idealistic, unselfconscious but aware of their beauty and high energy, excited, unknowing, eager to plunge in—and then the faltering. Older women circling, knowing, excited too but far too seasoned to thoughtlessly show their hands—also ashamed, to have such vivid emotions still, still at fifty and sixty and even seventy (especially seventy, when emotion was mainly what they had, and not so much physical touching). The older ones watching for the young one's moment of confusion, self-doubt, plain tiredness—who can live on ramen forever?—the older ones moved in like tired sharks, for the moment forgetting old wounds, closing their eyes and inhaling the smell of it, her fear and youth and inexperience, taking her in. Trying to convince her, each in their turn, that she needed someone to guide and settle her—that she couldn't be a free thing on her own, pulsating and laughing around them, evasive and elusive, ultimately, because of how she scarcely thought of them, because of how she could move forward innocent of all the ways they had once failed or been brought down, because she was still kind of innocent of all the ways it's possible to fail—'kind of' because she knew, but wasn't discouraged.

I watched Gigi watching conflicts and seductions. That was her main strength—her watchfulness, a quietude, the way she'd watched my face, caressed my hair, amused by everything I said. Elusive, in the end, but not so now. Because I saw her watching me.

"Are you okay?" was the first thing she

said, when, late after everyone else had gone, Gigi and I had ended up in bed.

"Don't know," I said.

There was a case or two that got to me. You can tell when it happens; a day or two when every conversation feels too bare, and it's all rules and plans and goals, and not feelings, because feelings would be too dangerous.

Like the box-cutter woman, whose face didn't make me flinch until I saw the photo where she smiled. Or maybe I had nightmares because I'd never actually met her. Only seen photographs on a lawyer's desk—a razor blade in thin lines on her face, eyes nearly swollen shut, lips bruised in a parody of a passionate kiss, welts on her neck, a broken nose. Her mouth mutilated at the corners, so that her smile would never be fully right again. I was frightened by the hot and cold rage that I felt. The day I'd seen her I wrote a note to the Mayor's commission, excoriating them for not doing enough, the Mayor too busy with his glamour life, his glamour wife a talking cable TV head. Gigi had scolded me furious in her office, pushing me up against the wall, unbuttoning my shirt, sticking her tongue into my mouth, but first saying: "Stop ticking everyone off. Get a massage or something, will you? Be different."

In Gigi's bed, days later, I cried.

She waited, patient.

"I can't be any different," I explained.

Being with Gigi, I could see in her a mirror of how well we both were aging. Brown didn't crack. Two wrinkles a piece—my two in between my brows (faint) and on the right forehead, consistent with my unpredictability, my unevenness. Gigi's wrinkles in deep "laugh lines" around her eyes, a mark of being Australian and imbibing all that sun. Our asses were about where they had been eight years ago. Our breasts slightly smaller. With her leg wrapped around my hip I could see that her thigh muscles were better, that she had gone hiking in Melbourne, at Twelve Apostles or some other tour-beautiful helicopter destination every weekend since being in high school. She had freckles.

Her eyes had lighter glints of brown than mine. My skin was darker—"more Dravidian," she liked to tease.

But there was tension all throughout my body, all the time. Whereas Gigi was alert but mostly relaxed, like she could be doing any job, running an advertising agency or yoga studio, managing a grocery store, whatever, it was work.

Different with me. I searched for relief, but couldn't imagine where it could come from. One of the old women at work—still young enough to wear expensive silks, her skin still with some sheen, her eyes still sharp enough to see and be attracted by the cruelty in my heart—she took me out for a martini once or twice, hopeful. But I couldn't take my mind away from how vulnerable her hands and wrists made her look—how both the skin and bones seemed breakable, how anyone could force themselves into her life and smash her up.

"Sorry," I'd said, moving away so our fingers didn't touch.

There was a guy or two, relentlessly poised over me, convinced he could make me forget fucking girls. Gigi didn't hear about them as I continued seeing her on and off, not answering when she talked about us living together. One guy was even Indian, Mahesh, "lord of it all" and with the slicked-back hair to match—but he made the memories even worse. He was an ER doc at UCSF, only vaguely interested in ever talking shop but when he'd found out what I had been doing with the Institute he tried to tell stories about roughed-up prostitutes, women with stab wounds, pregnant women with empty bellies, empty eyes.

For a short while, Mahesh seemed like he'd master me. Tall, smart enough to handle me roughly, he'd surprise me with some ice-cold remark, a smile that I realized was cruel only long afterwards. But he was proud of those stories, sincere in his way. Like Gigi, his job was only work to him—but he believed in it. Lacking in modesty he told me, serious, about the hundreds of people he saved in his short life. "It doesn't matter that I can't remember them," he said. "The thing is, I was there."

I didn't care about the whole dumb doctor bit. Of course, I did, because if I married him, I would be "set", as he often pointed out—more often than one might think, within a three-week hot, frenzied affair, given how little time was left for anything but bed. Dating a doctor made me feel guilty, for thinking of him as boring, even though his work was valuable. "You wouldn't give me a second look if I didn't eat you out," he grumbled. "Not even then," I said, realizing it was his gleaming hair I loved—the long black swag of it, all greaser pompadour, the thick reassuring mass I held when he went down and pleasured me, each time convincing me that he loved my taste. But he was thirty-eight to my twenty-eight, and told me he wanted to marry, thinking I'd quit the Institute, never suspecting what I was doing with Gigi.

Not that I would have guessed it myself. How, at age fifty, I would look up from a desk in a slightly-sunny room, some title on my wall with a small plaque, and realize that I'd built the Institute. How women whose names I couldn't remember—just like Mahesh barely remembered the identities of bodies he had saved—would press my hand or my shoulder, would read my books, would want to even sleep with me—even long after I'd committed to Gigi, after we'd gone back to Australia to live for years and I had helped her care for her mother, including at the end.

Hah. I wouldn't have guessed it, none of it. I didn't know how sweet the years added and subtracted would be—all those many years, the way I'd give them to my Gloria Geetanjali, my Gigi, unthinkingly, living each day as if I had the power to leave any second but knowing at the end of each one—sweaty from work, sex, building heavy things, or eventually, from hot flashes—that I wasn't going anywhere.

But there were hard times we got through, before I realized I would stay.

BORDERLAND

Creative Nonfiction

Illustrated by DefinitelyJenny
Written by Judson Merrill

Deer thrive in liminal spaces, the border-
lands at the edge of the woods. That's why
they're so prevalent in the suburbs, why you
see them along the side of the road, and why
they inhabit this coastal peninsula, where
the forest opens onto dune and marsh.
They have a wide field of vision well suit-
ed to these perimeters, but they struggle to
see things that aren't in motion. I knew this
vaguely, but spending time around deer,
facts like that—tidbits gleaned from nature
shows and old relatives—they crystallize
into something saltier than knowledge.

I was walking yesterday evening down
a dirt road winding along Maine's infinite
shore. I was looking west, toward the setting
sun, and didn't notice the doe on the east
side of the road until I was right next to her,
practically close enough to touch. Deer do
this sometimes, allow you to get surprisingly close even as they remain piqued, ready
to run. I froze in my tracks, half in surprise,
half in sympathetic response to her still-
ness. As she stood unmoving, staring at me
without seeming to see me, I remembered
that her non-motion vision was poor. And,
of course, she had no other conception of

vision. This was why she had frozen instead of bolted—in her instinctual way, she believed there was a decent chance that by not moving she had become invisible. It was sweet, really, this hope, and I felt bad being able to see her so clearly, to make out the grain of her russet coat.

As I stood watching her, thinking these things, I was myself completely still, wanting to prolong our

meeting. Which meant, then, that I had achieved what the doe had only hoped to achieve. I really was invisible. From her perspective, she'd been keeping a wary eye on me as I walked along the road and then I'd blinked out of sight. In the moment when I suddenly saw her, she suddenly didn't see me. Now we stood facing each other, each of us wondering if the other was going to move. If she moved, it would be to bound away, to disappear in an instant into the trees. If I moved, it would be to reappear, to lurch back into her field of vision.

This moment is another kind of liminal space, neither deer nor human, affording a glimpse, however fleeting and impossible, of the reality between us. Deer thrive in liminal spaces, and I wish this doe was having some equivalent moment, whatever that means for a deer, discerning for an instant life on the other side of the borderland. But the only reason we are standing so close, staring at each other across this dirt road, is because of her inability to even conceive of how I see the world, that I might be able to do something so incredible as watch her standing completely still in the last golden light of day.

CONTRIBUTORS

Chaya B.

lives in the US with her family, and had the inspiration for this piece daydreaming about communities she's been part of, including those fighting for social change.

Tyrese L. Coleman

is a writer, wife, mother, and attorney. She is also the fiction editor for *District Lit*, and an associate editor at *SmokeLong Quarterly*. A 2016 Kimbilio Fiction Fellow and a nonfiction scholar at Virginia Quarterly Review's 2016 Writer's Conference, her prose has appeared in several publications, including *PANK*, *Day One*, *Buzz-feed*, *Brevity*, *The Rumpus*, *Hobart*, listed in Wigleaf's Top 50 (very) short fictions, and forthcoming at *The Kenyon Review*. She can be reached at tyresecoleman.com.

Chrissy Curtin

is a professional Illustrator and portrait artist. She is also Irish. Her main focus is editorial work, but she loves making all types of illustration. She works from her home studio in Ireland with her two dogs, Lady & Moose!

DefinitelyJenny

Illustrator//Book Lover//Cat Video Addict
Currently based in High Wycombe, she is an illustrator

with a strong interest in graphic design, particularly in layout and publishing.

Kim Herbst

is a half-Chinese freelance illustrator who spent time in Taipei, Tokyo, New Jersey, Baltimore, and Brooklyn before heading out to reside in San Francisco. Her work has been featured in newspapers, magazines, children's educational materials, and gallery shows.

Tee Indawongse

is a final year medical student at the University of Queensland, Australia. She has a passion for women's health, but in her free time, has a powerful drive to write something worth reading. She is the 2016 recipient of SLQ's Young Writers Award for writers aged 18–25 years. She has previously been published in *Voiceworks, Tincture, Litro Online* and elsewhere.

Jess E. Jelsma

is a doctoral student in creative writing at the University of Cincinnati and holds an MFA in prose from the University of Alabama. Her previous work has appeared or is forthcoming in *The Chicago Tribune, Indiana Review, The Rumpus, The Normal School, Post Road*, and various other publications. She is currently at work on a collaborative, serialized nonfiction podcast with Matt Jones, and can be found online at jessejelsma.com.

Matt Jones

is a recent graduate of the University of Alabama MFA program and his prose has appeared or is forthcoming in *The Atlantic, Clarkesworld, The Journal, Post Road, Slice*

Magazine, and various other publications. He currently teaches at the University of Cincinnati and Xavier University and can be found online at mattjonesfiction.com.

Franz Lang

is an Italian illustrator creating colourful worlds of quirky characters from his studio in East London. Instagram: @franz_lang_

Michael Lehman

studied writing at a state university, worked for newspapers, and lives in the mountains. His essay from the Standing Rock pipeline resistance, titled 'Plymouth Rock Standing on its Head,' appears in the current issue of *Camas* magazine.

Alistair Mackay

grew up in Johannesburg, South Africa. He has an MA degree in politics from Edinburgh University and worked as a digital marketer in Cape Town for many years, two experiences that provided inspiration for this story. He is currently based in New York City and is a Columbia University MFA candidate (2017). He can be found online at www.alistaircharlesmackay.com

Judson Merrill

grew up in Maine, studied literature and writing at Brown University, and received his MFA from Brooklyn College. His work has appeared or is forthcoming in *The Iowa Review*, *The Southampton Review*, *Unstuck*, *McSweeney's Internet Tendency*, and other publications. He has recently been an Artist in Residence at Millay Colony, Ox-

Bow, Lighthouse Works, and Guild Hall.

Yolanda Oreiro aka Mitucami Mituca
is a Spanish illustrator, currently based in Barcelona. She is the in-house illustrator and a guest editor at *Penny*.

David Mohan
has been published in *PANK*, *Necessary Fiction*, *Word Riot*, *SmokeLong Quarterly*, *Matchbook* and *The Chattahoochee Review*. He has been nominated for The Pushcart Prize.

Sophie Page
is a mixed media 3d illustrator and RISD grad based in NYC, from Conway MA. sophiegenevapage.com ~ @ladle_gull

Plum
is an illustration collective based in Brooklyn, NY.

Katy Shay
is finishing up her MFA at the University of Miami-Ohio and has a sixteen year old cat. Her work has previously been published in *Word Riot* and *The Huron River Review*.

Michelle Spokes'
piece surfaced during yoga practice. The study and teaching of both yoga and writing have revealed to her that not only the mind, but the body, too, can carry memories, often in a symbolic way. Her work appears in the *Oyez Review; siren; Fireweed; BellyDance.One;* the anthology, *A Wake Up Call*, edited by Jan Phillips; and *7 Veils*, from

Hay House press.

Renata Srpcanska

was born in Macedonia and lived there until she moved to London, where she learned photography and theater. She studied illustration at the School of Art and Design of Tarragona. Her constant is fantasy, intimacy and a gentle and delicate chromatic fan.

Sarah Tinsley

is a writer, teacher, runner and drummer who lives in London. She is prone to musing over gender issues and eating cheese. She won the Segora Short Story competition in 2015 and was Highly Acclaimed in the Aurora Short Fiction Competition in 2016. Her short fiction, reviews and blogs have been published on a variety of platforms. You can find her on Twitter @sarahertinsley or on her blog at sarahtinsley.com.

Emily Zasada

has had a story previously published in *Flock* (formerly *Fiction Fix*). She's a fan of jazz, seventies music, and the color orange. Originally from Maryland, she now lives in Northern Virginia with her husband, son, and two highly opinionated beagle mixes.

Please scan a QR code, or type a web address, into your internet-enabled device, and you will be taken to the online home of a story. We invite you to add your comments and ideas or share the link with friends. We look forward to hearing from you!

Between the Wish  bit.ly/ penny0304	**body memory**  bit.ly/ penny0306	**Borderland**  bit.ly/ penny0312	**Café**  bit.ly/ penny0301
Chrysalis  bit.ly/ penny0310	**Dear Nnamdi**  bit.ly/ penny0302	**Queen of Wings**  bit.ly/ penny0309	**The Free Clinic**  bit.ly/ penny0303
The King of the Jungle  bit.ly/ penny0305	**When the Rains Come**  bit.ly/ penny0308	**The Balloon Loan**  bit.ly/ penny0307	**Sex with Indians**  bit.ly/ penny0311

www.ingramcontent.com/pod-product-compliance
Lightning Source LLC
Chambersburg PA
CBHW072304130726